Moss could not turn back—even if he wanted

It was too late to stay in one spot. It was too late to be careful. It was too late to mark my own trail. A thought arose from somewhere in the center of my body and spread like the circles that grow in water from the splash of a rock: this was not a game I could stop whenever I wanted. It *was* dangerous. I *could* get hurt. I might never find my way home, and if I tried to go back, guessing the way I had come, it was likely that I would become more lost. I would be looking for something that could no longer be found.

MICHAEL DORRIS

GUESTS

SCHOLASTIC INC.

New York Toronto London Auckland Sydney
Mexico City New Delhi Hong Kong

ISBN 0-439-14061-7

Published by Scholastic Inc., 555 Broadway, New York, NY 10012, by arrangement with Hyperion Books for Children, an imprint of Buena Vista Books, Inc. SCHOLASTIC and associated logos are trademarks and/or registered trademarks of Scholastic Inc.

24 23 22 21 20 19 18 17 16 15 14 13   7 8 9/0

Printed in the U.S.A.   40

First Scholastic printing, October 1999

This book is set in 12-point Palatino.

For Persia, who read it first
For Pallas, who thought Running Woman
was "fabulus"
For Aza, whose verve inspired
And for Louise,
who, as ever, turned the key

GUESTS

CHAPTER ONE

 The day began with an accident. I was playing with a string of old wampum—I knew I was not supposed to touch it—when it broke apart, scattering beads on the ground. Wampum belts were important things, taken out and passed around by old people on special occasions—like today—and now, as the light through the smoke hole in the roof turned from black to gray, and the first birds of

1

morning began to greet each other, I had started the day off wrong.

My father propped himself on one elbow, squinted to see what I was trying to pick up so quietly.

"I'll find them all," I whispered.

He shook his head once, very firmly, when he saw what had happened, then combed his hair with his fingers, pulling it back from his forehead tighter than he needed to.

"I'll fix them exactly as they were. Better. Even prettier."

My father located one pale white bead of mollusk shell that had stopped within his reach, turned it over in his palm. "No," he said softly so as not to disturb my mother. "We'll ask your grandfather if he remembers how they were set. You don't understand, Moss. The design held a story from long ago, a story that took place one way and no other. If the arrangement is confused, even a little bit, so is the story along with it."

I stared at the white and purple beads, pleading with them to roll back as they had been. I closed my eyes, tried to picture the full belt, but the patterns blurred in my mind. I couldn't return to the moment when they had been right, when the story that they remembered had still matched the truth.

Later, when the sun had cleared the grassy bluffs that separate our village from the sea, my father and I carried the beads in a sweetgrass basket to my grandfather's house—wide and round, built at the base of a pine tree. Its bark sides still held the night's dew and were dark brown against the cushion of soft green needles on the ground.

Grandmother was already out in the fields, but Grandfather was sitting before the fire. When I showed him the basket, he studied the contents for many slow minutes, now and then stirring the beads with his strong fingers. Finally, he sighed. "They are once again just carved shells," he said. "All those years I've seen them without seeing them. I should have paid more attention."

"But it's not your fault!" I cried. Grandfather seemed so disappointed in himself, and it wasn't fair. "*I* lost our story." My mind fought with itself— I didn't want to think about what I had done, but not thinking about it made me think about nothing else.

3

Standing behind me, my father put his hand on my shoulder. His touch was light as a breeze that blows before rain, and I leaned back into it to feel it harder.

Grandfather nodded, then gave the basket four shakes, one for each direction, causing the beads to leap and dance among themselves. He looked up at me, his face serious.

"Now you owe us a story, Moss," he said, and handed the basket back into my arms.

"What kind of a story?" I owned no interesting stories. There was nothing special about what I ate or what I saw or where I went or what I did when I got there.

Grandfather made his eyes go round, as if already listening, as if surprised by what he was hearing. "How should I know?" he asked. "It could be anything, and there is no hurry. Just make sure it's worth the work it will take for someone to sew these old shells together in a new way."

＊＊＊

When we got home, Mother gave me a cold corn cake from yesterday's dinner and sent me outside so that she could prepare for tonight's feast.

"Amuse yourself," she told me. "And if you want to be helpful later on, bring back some firewood. There's never enough, once I get started with cooking for a big group."

I sat in the shade of a large maple tree, its leaves orange and purple against the blue autumn sky. Almost immediately my older cousin, Cloud, joined me. He was never far away when there was food, and without waiting for him to ask I broke off a piece of my cake and handed it to him.

"I should save my appetite," he said as he finished it off in two gulps and then looked longingly toward what I had kept for myself. Cloud had grown tall this year, almost as big as my uncle—his father—and his constant eating was a joke in our family.

I held the rest of the cake up in front of me, as if using it to block the sun from my eyes, and let Cloud wish.

"When are you going to tell me about your away time?" I asked him, as I had done almost every day through the summer.

He couldn't take his eyes off the food—we both knew it would be late afternoon before the big meal started—but he shook his head.

"You'll have to find out for yourself." He was proud of what he knew and I didn't. "It's different for everyone, so no one can prepare you."

"Don't make yourself so important," I said.

"Be patient, little cousin." Cloud smiled at the remains of my corn cake so hopefully that I bit off half, chewed, and swallowed.

"You promised, last spring before you left, that when you came back, no matter what, you would tell me everything that had happened to you."

"I know," Cloud admitted. "It's just that you . . . I . . . well, you can't. . . . All I can say is, when it's your turn just open your mind and watch what you see."

"Open my mind and watch what I see." I repeated Cloud's words slowly to prod him into continuing. Nobody would ever talk about their away time, yet mine was all I could think about. After this winter I was supposed to go off to the woods alone and somehow learn important new things about myself

—a new name, what work I should do as a man—and I had no notion how to get ready or what to expect.

"That's it?" I asked finally, when Cloud didn't add any more information.

"You'll understand when the time comes."

I was tired of people pointing out what I didn't understand yet. According to my father, I didn't understand yet how wampum belts worked. According to Cloud, I didn't understand yet about away time. At night I didn't understand my own dreams. During the day I didn't understand why certain girls whose names I barely knew laughed among themselves whenever I walked past: they would act normal one minute and then turn odd the next. And today, especially on the day I lost the wampum story, I didn't understand why we had to have guests.

***

I gave Cloud the rest of my breakfast—maybe tomorrow he would say more—and stayed where I was when he wandered off to follow the smell of roasting squash. After a while, my father came out of our family's house and started to work in the clearing at the center of the village. He was finishing a canopy of saplings and reed grass, a shelter where we would all eat together later on if the weather was nice. Seeing him, my mind filled with old objections. I couldn't forget an argument with my parents that had been left unfinished, an argument about the strangers that my father had invited—all on his own, when he'd met one of them in the woods—to share our harvest meal. I got up and went over to join him.

"Why?" I insisted, as if no time had passed between last night's talk and this moment. "Why today?"

My father stopped binding the frame together with a rope of twisted grapevine. He pulled a breath through his teeth, then spoke his words carefully, each a step following the other up a steep path. I had put the exact same question to him more than once yesterday, and he had not been able to explain his reasons to me. The final time I asked, in the dark, he pretended to be asleep. Well, he was awake now.

"Because. They. Are. Hungry." He wiped his forehead with the back of his hand and looked around, hoping someone would come by to interrupt us.

"*We've* been hungry before," I reminded him. "Nobody invited us to come ruin *their* only-once-in-a-whole-year special day."

"Don't you wish that during those times someone *had* invited us? Moss, it's simply the proper thing to do." My father nodded encouragingly as if this argument settled the issue. When I didn't nod also, he lowered his eyebrows, made a scary face, and ran his thumb down the length of my nose the way he used to do in play when I was a small boy. Then, this game had made me laugh—but not this morning. This morning I jerked my face away, left his hand waving in the air between us. This was not some little problem he could make go away with a joke for babies.

He sighed. "You'll understand when you're older."

Just what I expected him to say.

"I won't," I promised him, then gave his own word back to him. "Instead, I'll remember how this year never *properly* ended, how next year never *prop-*

erly began, because we failed to *properly* celebrate the bridge between them."

I shot a glance to gauge my father's reaction, but he had closed his eyes and made himself invisible to me. His mouth had become a thin straight line and his nostrils were wide.

I stepped close to him, stood on tiptoe. "My mind won't change just because you ignore me," I whispered directly into his ear.

He opened one eye. "I might as well be talking with your grandfather."

Grandfather was well known for being stubborn in his ideas. For instance, you couldn't convince him to cross a frozen river until he had found deer tracks on the center ice. You couldn't substitute a single word when repeating an old story. You had to go to sleep facing east so that you would be ready to greet the sun when it returned.

Only two days before, I had asked Grandfather how he felt about the strangers' coming, but when he began to answer he had gotten stuck between two "shoulds": we *should* hold the feast exactly the way we always had before, and guests who came in

10

peace *should* always be offered the first serving of food—even if you didn't much like them and hoped they would soon go home. When Grandfather couldn't choose in favor of one without choosing against the other, he gave up and spent an endless afternoon showing me how to carve fishhooks from twigs.

I tried one last appeal to my father. "These people are not our relatives. We don't even know their names. We can't talk with them because they speak a language no one but they understand. They make me uncomfortable with their oddness."

"Me, too." My father always surprised me when he spoke to me without acting like a father, almost as though I were another grown-up. I didn't know what to say, and so he filled the pause that followed with a big rock I couldn't move. "Yet we can't turn them away. An invitation once given cannot be taken back."

I shook my head in irritation, moved across the clearing to the doorway of our house, where my mother was cooking—but not before my father called after me. "For once we have enough. What

11

else would you have us . . . *properly* . . . do? Does food taste better if some of it is left uneaten?"

✳✳✳

"It's not the feeding them that bothers me," I explained to my mother. She was stewing meat, swirling the broth with her wooden ladle to keep it from sticking to the hard-sided kettle the strangers had traded in exchange for our extra furs. "Why couldn't we just send them some corn—as much as they needed? Then they could eat it at their own house. They'd probably like that better."

"Isn't there anything else for you to talk about?" Mother asked me. "All you have to do is make room in the eating circle, be polite. *I* had to harvest the crops and now have to cook them. Shall we switch places? I'll feel sorry for myself, you work."

Being just *us*, our family, our village, all together, meant nothing even to her, nothing to anyone except me. Didn't they notice? People acted so differently in front of outsiders—so stiff and shy, never smiling or playing a joke. We couldn't enjoy ourselves. We would have to stand outside our own words, listen to ourselves to make sure we were *proper*.

Mother stopped what she was doing and looked into my eyes. "You're behaving selfishly, Moss," she said in a more serious tone. "Hospitality isn't unusual, something you choose to do or not, it's ordinary." Her voice softened. "It's like sleeping so that you will be rested when you wake. It's like gathering wood so that you can have a fire when the snow comes. It's like making pemmican instead of eating all the meat immediately. Like listening to good advice."

I glanced around the dim corners of the house as if searching for something I had forgotten. I was stuck, a tug rope pulled equally by both sides, suspended over mud.

My mother was watching my face, waiting to see some leap in my thoughts, but I pretended not to notice and finally she went back to her stirring. I felt her disappointment too strongly to think about it, yet I knew she would not become angry with me. I was the only one of her children who had not fallen ill with the coughing sickness, the only one left for her. Sometimes that was hard for both of us.

"Moss?"

"If they come, I won't stay." My words were louder than they had to be, louder than they should have been.

Inside the pot the chunks of venison meat followed each other through the water in a slowing circle. Bubbles rose to the surface, and the warm smell of soup crept over me.

"We will miss you," my mother said at last.

"Maybe they'll get lost on the way, change their minds." But they wouldn't. They were hungry, my father had told us.

Mother hummed a corn song, shifting her weight to the rhythm. Her hair, held back from her face by a band of tanned deerskin, gleamed like still water in moonlight. A pale scar, thin and crooked as a strip of raspberry branch, ran through her lower lip and halfway down her chin. That was why her name was Two Halves, the same way my name came from the fact that when I was a baby I wanted to be next to my mother all the time. People teased me, even now, that I stayed as close to her as moss to a rock.

I waited for a moment, listening to the song, wanting today to start over and be like it should have been. I wanted to joke and dance and taste the chewy orange pumpkin, the sweet red beans, the rich meat. I wanted to listen to Grandfather's familiar stories and to stay awake late, my head against his side, as the fire died down and we watched together for the stars that formed the outline of the bear to rise. I wanted this year to be just like last year and the year before that, as far back as I could remember.

But the guests would spoil everything, even blur my memory of other feasts. I wished they had never left wherever they came from before they got here. I wished they would return there again and forget the trail through the sea that they had followed. I wished they would grow their own food, trap their own furs, keep their pots and thin cloth and hardheaded hammers. I wished for just one more right time before things began to change.

CHAPTER TWO

 The light from the doorway was suddenly blocked as my father entered.

"Were you able to reason with him?" he asked my mother, as if I weren't there.

"Oh yes," she said. "Moss listens closely to me these days. But now he tells me that he'd rather leave the village than stay and help us entertain the guests and make the best of the day."

My father reached back to squeeze the muscles behind his neck. Finally, he looked over to me.

"So. What should you never forget to bring when you go away to the forest?"

All right, I thought. I can play this game.

"A knife," I guessed.

He shook his head.

"A hatchet to cut wood?"

More shaking.

"Flints—to make fire?"

"Those are all good suggestions," my father agreed, "yet none of them is the *most* important." He settled himself comfortably and waited for me to continue. He seemed so content with being wiser than me that I spoke before I thought about what I was saying.

"Your *father*," I said. "You should always bring your father because he'll know *everything* you should do."

My father pulled his head back as if a hummingbird had suddenly whirred before his nose. He glanced over at my mother, who wouldn't meet his eyes, so at last he turned back to me. The air was

17

smoky, and I couldn't be sure of his expression.

"What a fine answer," he said. His voice was even, pretending to be itself even though it was something else. "But why *only* to the forest? Perhaps you should take your father with you when you play games with your friends. When you swim in the lake. Perhaps, someday, when you marry, you should take your father to live with you and your wife as well!"

"How helpful," my mother said, and then addressed my father as if she had just had a new idea. "Perhaps you should have kept *your* father with *you*. Think of all the good advice he could give us every day. And of course you always agree with his opinions—when you are able to coax them from him."

"I'm *not* like my father," my father said. Now he was talking only to my mother, not me, and he was no longer so comfortable.

"Not at all," my mother agreed. "Not a bit. Of course not. Your father has answers for every question and is never wrong, never needs to compromise. Sometimes, however, he may forget to laugh at himself."

There was a silence between my parents so pure that I listened to the heat from the cooking fire. I couldn't decide whether they were arguing or joking with each other, and I don't think they could tell, either. After a pause, my mother tipped the balance.

"Besides," she bent toward me and whispered, "if you were to take your father with you to the forest, what would I do without him? Who would warm me at night? Who would build the canopy for the feast? Who would deal with the guests when they arrive? You'll have to take something else."

"Rope," my father said. He sounded relieved, glad to have the right answer. "A line made from braided bark or strong reeds. A long coil."

"Rope?" my mother and I asked at the same time.

"With rope you can make a trap or the roof pole for a tent of twigs. With rope you can fish, or drag heavy wood. With rope you can fashion a sling or bind a wound or measure distance or hang something from a high tree so you will always know where you are."

"Rope is useful not only in the forest," my mother said. "With rope you can also tie your husband to the house post so he'll never think to go far away."

"You don't need rope for that." My father smiled and filled his bowl so that he could taste her soup. They were both happy with each other again, and our house had suddenly become too small for me. For my parents, I had already left before I was actually gone.

✳✳✳

I slipped through our doorway and followed the path that weaves the village together. The sun was small in the sky, its light tinted by the leaves that hung low from the limbs of maple trees or scattered on the ground. The air tasted like the smoke of many green cooking fires, and everywhere there was the sound of women talking, of children playing, of men calling questions to each other. Because I was doing nothing to get ready for the feast, I was free to observe like a visitor, like a bird resting his wings on a rooftop before flying away toward the south.

I swept my gaze from right to left, waiting for a sight to hold my attention in one place, but what I saw going on around me suddenly seemed . . . old. It was as if I were watching a family of beavers repairing their dam, diving in and out of the water, chewing wood, brushing past each other in their hurry to complete jobs they had performed a hundred times before. How many logs, over the years, had my mother fed into her cooking fire? How many times had my father repaired his frayed bowstring? How often were baskets filled only to be emptied, emptied only to be filled?

Even this feast, this final taste of summer before we had to remember the length of the coming winter and eat only in small portions, was the echo of something that had happened and happened and happened. Each autumn harvest we stuffed our stomachs with the same kinds of food, heard the same words, sang the same songs. If the weather was rainy or snowy we would move indoors. If it was warm we would stay outdoors until the fireflies burned out. In every direction as far as I could see I looked and looked and learned nothing that I didn't already know, found nothing that made me curious.

Wait. There, behind the low skirt of a cedar tree across the clearing, I sensed a quietness to match my own, a calm pool among the swirling waters, and I narrowed my eyes to see more closely. A girl named Trouble was staring back at me, her head tipped to one side, her hands clasped together before her dress. Her expression said that she was as surprised to find me as I was to find her. We were like two deer, each strayed from a different herd, who discover each other at a stream and instantly realize that the forest is bigger than either of them had ever imagined.

I tried to remember what I knew about Trouble. She was about my age, tall, kin in some way to my mother's Turtle Clan—which meant that she was not related to my grandfather, my father, or me, and that she lived on the other side of the village with people that I'd see every day but mostly didn't know. I'd politely greet their elders when I encountered them, sometimes play with the boys my age—but not the girls, because a long time off, when I got married, my mother said it would probably be to one of them.

"A husband and wife need to be new to each other," my mother explained one day after she had come home from visiting her brother's house for some kind of ceremony to which I had not been invited.

"Was that how it was with you and my father?" I asked her, even though I couldn't imagine a time when my parents hadn't been themselves. Just thinking about such things made me uncomfortable.

"It still is," she said, almost to herself, and looked back across the clearing as if the distance to the other side of the village was very long.

Of course, stories were told about Trouble, as stories were told about every person in the village. She was supposed to be a fast runner, quick as a dragonfly. When she was small she had never cried, even when she was hungry. My grandmother still marveled at this whenever her own grandchildren were too noisy, when they yelled out their wishes and never made you guess what they wanted.

"She's a thoughtful one," my grandmother would nod, making me feel as though I was not thoughtful at all. "That's the way to be."

"If she was so easy, why did her parents name her Trouble?" I wanted to know.

My grandmother had brightened. "Exactly! She was so easy they could afford to give her a difficult name. You would never call a small child Small, a heavy child Fat. A name reminds, it doesn't describe. It can be the opposite of the truth, or something in between, like a light that casts a shadow."

"Then why am I Moss?" I asked.

"Because it would have been unkind to call you Crybaby," my grandmother said, and covered her mouth with her hand to hide her laugh.

Now, as I watched her, Trouble still looked thoughtful. Her lips were pressed together. Her chin was raised as if in answer to an unfair accusation. Her arms were crossed, and she held her elbows with her hands. Her eyes were two small fires shining from the gloom.

When at last she moved toward the end of the village where the land sloped down into the deeper woods, I couldn't help it, I followed. I would chase after Trouble until I found out where that took me. At least, I told myself, whatever happened next had not occurred before.

✳✳✳

"Leave. Me. Alone." Trouble was out of breath, and her words had to fight their way from her mouth.

"Why?" It was true she was fast, and I struggled to slow my own breathing so it would not betray how hard I had run to catch up.

She waded her feet into the ground cover of leaves, and a rustle filled the air. We were far enough

24

from the village so that the forest closed around our ears like water below the surface of a summer lake. Everywhere the shadows were bright, flickering with the smallest shift of overhanging branches.

"Why?" I repeated when she refused to look at me. In my voice I recognized the question I had earlier asked my father, and I didn't want another "you wouldn't understand."

Without waiting for Trouble to answer, I said, "Never mind. I probably wouldn't understand if you told me why you came out here. I don't under-stand anything today." I sat down, then lay back, put my hands under my head and stared up at the sky, motionless as a drop of water on a flat rock.

The normal flow of time hesitated.

"What do you mean?" Trouble asked at last, try-ing not to sound too curious.

I rolled to my side, glanced to where she stood, then past her, out across the leaves. "Nothing." All my thoughts seemed to bounce into each other, to play tag with me when I tried to grab them.

The silence widened. I felt her sit next to me.

"I know what you mean," she whispered.

There were leaves below me and beside me and

25

above me. I was lost in a huge, high-roofed room of mixing reds and browns and purples and greens, some bright, some dim, each shading into the other to create one enormous color, too big for any single name to describe. My mind expanded to fill the space, to become part of it. I had spoken without planning what to say, and what I had said made no sense, even to me. If *I* didn't know what I meant, how could she?

"My mother thinks I'm lazy," I said, offering an excuse.

"My sisters say I love to fight with them," Trouble confided.

"My father shuts his eyes when I try to talk seriously."

"My father . . . ," Trouble began, and then stopped.

"Even my cousin Cloud," I went on, "who also used to be my friend, won't keep his promises. Half the time people treat me as though I'm younger than I am and the other half they want me to be older. It's either 'Think for yourself' or 'Do what I tell you and don't ask questions.'"

I realized I had been speaking with a shouting

voice, because when I stopped the sound continued to float in the air, then settled like dew on every surface. In embarrassment, I darted a glance at Trouble to judge her reaction. Her eyebrows were lowered into lines sharp as lances. She had gathered a small hill of leaves into her lap and was neatly tearing them apart, one by one, following the paths of their seams. I picked up a stick and began to drill a hole into the soft ground. The trees seemed very high, the quiet very crisp, the distance back to this morning very far.

"I . . . ," I began. What would I hear myself say next?

"You, you, you," Trouble broke in.

I was angry that she should tease me when I had just admitted thoughts to her I had never before expressed, even to myself.

I concentrated on turning my stick, and after a moment I heard the leaves begin to tear once more.

"I'm sorry," Trouble said. "I'm a terrible person, as bad as Shale."

Shale was a boy I didn't like. Nobody did. He made fun of everything and yet he was rarely funny.

"No you aren't," I said. "Shale eats bugs."

27

"He *does*?" Trouble was delighted to learn this news.

We looked at each other, then quickly turned away. It was not polite to stare too long at another person's smile.

✳✳✳

After a while, I asked, "Why do you say you're a terrible person?"

Trouble shook her head, thought about whether she should answer, then decided. "I'm never satisfied."

I nodded slowly. It was as if I was hearing a thought from inside my own head. Before I could tell her this amazing fact, she continued.

"My parents used to admire that about me," she said. "They laughed when nothing was too much for me, made up tests—picked more berries than they thought I could eat, let me swim until they were sure I'd be tired, told me scary stories at night until anyone else would have begged them to stop."

"My grandmother calls you thoughtful," I told her. "Not terrible."

Trouble's face briefly tightened with pleasure,

but then she shrugged. "That's what my mother used to say, too. But no more."

"What . . . ?" I began, but Trouble interrupted.

"Why are you out here today? Won't they be looking for you before the big meal starts?"

I considered telling her the whole story, but a better idea jumped into my mouth. "I'm going on my away time—to find out who I really am."

Trouble frowned. "Boys do that in the spring, when it's safe," she said. "This time of year you could get caught in bad weather and never find your way out of the woods."

She was right, of course, but I couldn't back down. "You have to go when you have to go." I tried to sound as knowledgeable and superior as Cloud. "A man cannot pick when."

The word "man" felt odd when I used it about myself, as if I were impersonating someone big and powerful.

"Tell the truth," Trouble said, not believing me.

"It *is* the truth," I answered. "And anyway, why are you here? You're a girl." I gestured into the woods. "Snakes, bears."

Trouble shook her head. "I come here all the time, every day. It's the place I go when I need to hear myself."

I looked at her. She wasn't bragging—she actually *did* come out here by herself, something I had never even thought of doing. I wanted to ask her if she wasn't afraid, if she didn't worry, if she ever came at night. I wanted to ask if she minded about guests being invited for the feast. I wanted to ask if she had heard anything about away times, because somehow I knew, if she had, she would tell me. I wanted to ask her more questions than I ever wondered about before, more questions than I could think of quickly but was sure were waiting to present themselves. They crowded together, pushing each other aside to be first, and they got stuck the way people do when they all try to squeeze through a small doorway at the same time.

"You don't have a knife," Trouble noticed. "You don't even have a string of rawhide to make a snare." She was almost about to be impressed, I could tell, and I didn't want to disappoint her.

"I'm going with nothing," I said, braver than I felt.

"You're bluffing," Trouble insisted. But she was beginning to be not sure, and so I had no choice. I stood up, took a long breath, shut my eyes, and walked alone into the forest.

CHAPTER THREE

 The world disappeared. Everything that had mattered, that had seemed so necessary before the leaves closed behind me, now made no difference. There was nobody to complain to, nobody to resist. There was nothing I had to do, nothing I was forbidden. Every step took me farther away from all I knew. Every branch I pushed past was a shutting gate. Every turn I made to the right

32

or left had never been made before. I couldn't see more than a few feet in any direction and so all choices were equal. I was heading for nowhere, for anywhere, for everywhere, but there was no certainty that I would ever arrive at the place where I should go—or that I'd recognize it if I did.

All the usual guides were gone or confusing. From the dim light, it could have been early morning or late afternoon or a night with a bright full moon. There was no beaten trail to follow, no murmur of conversation to draw me, no rule to keep or break. All my knowledge of "how to" or "how not," all that experience had taught me, all the boundaries that had seemed so safe or so annoying, were now memories, dream stories that turned to mist at daybreak.

I had not taken many steps before I realized what a bad idea this had been. I didn't care what Trouble thought of me. I didn't care if she told Shale, who would tell everyone else. I didn't care about the guests.

"Trouble," I called. "Where are you?" Her voice would be the stream that would lead me back.

There was no answer, only the hollowness of the

33

inside of a shell. "Trouble!" I tried again, this time louder, cupping my palms around my mouth. When there was no reply, I turned in circles, shouting then listening into each spot I faced. "Don't joke me," I pleaded.

I studied the ground and could not figure out the path I had just taken. I had left no tracks, and none of the half-bare trees looked more or less familiar than the others. In such a short walk I had traveled deeper, beyond any range I had imagined possible, and for the first time in my life there was no one to help me, no one to come if I called—yet somehow that insight did not connect with what I did next.

"HELP!" I yelled again and again. "HELPHELPHELPHELP!" I heard a scurry in the dense bushes behind me, turned and fled from it, dodging trees, leaping over the ground whenever it dipped, thrashing through tall grass that tossed seeds every which way as I knocked against its dry blooms. I ran without pause or purpose, ran as if I were being hunted, ran like a racing fire, until finally I tripped, sprawled on my stomach. Panting, I turned over.

Birds must have been making noise before and

stopped at my outburst, because suddenly I noticed a new level of silence. And here's the odd thing: as each normal solution to my predicament occurred to me and then had to be dismissed, as the size of my own stupidity—first for putting myself in this situation and then for not knowing what to do once I was here—settled over me like the shadow of a rain cloud, other parts of me seemed magically to get smarter. I saw details I had never previously noticed: the shape of bark as it folded into gnarls, the veins in rock, the shimmer and sparkle of a spiderweb. I felt the earth under me, solid and steady. I smelled not just the ordinary musty odor of the forest, but many flavors—the tang of mint, the rot of logs, the sweet sing of water.

My mind shed its weight, abandoned its effort to divide the tumble of my senses into words or ideas. I opened my mouth, opened my eyes, opened my hands, opened my ears. I was a house whose walls had fallen down, all at the same time, during a thunderstorm: the outside and the inside rushed together, became one place. In the mix, every object, every noise, every movement was bright and sharp and startling. I had never been so awake. A strong wind blew straight through me, washing out the dust, leaving me clean.

✳✳✳

I awoke without remembering having been asleep. The forest was as I had left it, busy with itself, taking no notice of my presence. Had a long time passed? Was my mother waiting for my return? Had Trouble passed on the news of my away time? Was my father searching for me near the place where Trouble and I had talked? Had the guests arrived? Were they now fed and satisfied?

The thought of food announced to me that I was very hungry, as if I had not eaten for many days. My lips were dry. I felt chilled and stood up stiffly, missing the warmth of my mother's fire. The problem remained: I didn't know where I was or what I was supposed to do to find out. I tried to remember everything I had ever heard about the forest—warnings people had exchanged while I barely listened, too interested in something else. I especially tried to recall bad mistakes people had made when they were lost, and of course the first bit of advice that came back to me was that you were supposed to stay where you were and let yourself be found. The absolute worst thing you could do was panic.

Like I had just done.

✳✳✳

I didn't have a knife. I didn't have a hatchet. I didn't have flints. I didn't have rope. I didn't even have warm clothing, and the air was cold against the skin of my face and hands. I wished I *had* brought my father with me, or, better than that, I wished I was still in the village, full of good food, safe, and surrounded by relatives and friends. I stood very still, squinted my eyes, and imagined every person I would see there. I imagined what they were wearing, what they were doing, what they were saying. It was all so real that when I stopped and found myself still surrounded by dark-trunked trees, I was not just afraid, I was also determined.

What should I do? I had never concentrated quite this hard about anything before—but then, I had never needed to. This situation was different and new in every way, and my mind stretched to capture all the loose ideas, ran to gather them before they danced so far apart they could not talk to each other.

It was too late to stay in one spot. It was too late to be careful. It was too late to mark my own trail. A thought arose from somewhere in the center of my body and spread like the circles that grow in water from the splash of a rock: this was not a game I could stop whenever I wanted. It *was* dangerous. I *could* get hurt. I might never find my way home, and if I tried to go back, guessing the way I had come, it was likely that I would become more lost. I would be looking for something that could no longer be found.

Going back was just . . . going back. If I succeeded in finding my way, I would only be where I had started, and all that had taken place since I stepped alone into the forest would be gone from my life, like a great storm whose puddles dried up so completely that you couldn't find where they'd been and so were never sure *if* they had been. Going back was like saying no after I had already said yes.

If I went back now, or tried to, I would always be Moss, the boy who stayed a boy, to myself as well as to everyone else. If I went back now, I would be going back *farther* than the place where I had started, and I might never be brave enough to leave again, because giving up would always be in front of me as a thing I might do.

Since I couldn't go back, since I couldn't stay where I was, I had to go forward. The way home, if there was one, was to walk ahead, to discover a new road that would belong to no one but me, to find my way out through a different door than the one I had entered. And so, not because I wanted to but because it was the only possibility, I stepped into the forest for a second time, but now my eyes were open.

***

As I walked, I listened at first to the crunch of my own feet on the fallen needles of the tall white pines. The wide trunks tapered upward to a roof of branches so crowded together that a squirrel could walk from tree to tree without leaping. The air was like a cave, cool and solemn, scratched by the brush of my legs as I wove between the short plants like a sewing bone. All the while I was alert for sounds that had no part of me in them, sounds that bubbled, steam from a pot, sounds whose names I had yet to say.

Cloud's words suddenly came back to me.

39

"Open your mind and watch what you see," he had advised, so I decided to try it. Some stories claimed that during the away time a great animal or a high-flying bird—a bear or a wolf, an eagle or a hawk—might suddenly appear as a guide to help a boy learn about his true self, to show him the way he should follow. Perhaps now that would happen for me.

I stared at nothing, resisted blinking until my eyes went stiff, and waited. And waited. And. Waited. I tried to keep ordinary concerns—like how hungry I felt, how tired, how thirsty, how lonely, how scared—far away, and concentrated on following Cloud's instructions. I am ready, I told myself. I am ready *now*.

Ready for what? an old-lady voice demanded.

"To be grown up."

I had answered a question that I had sensed rather than heard aloud—and was shocked at the sound of my own words. Who was I speaking to?

"Is somebody here?" I called out.

Go home. You woke me up.

The complaint that formed inside my mind was so sharp and grouchy that I frowned, then crouched down low and looked around. The forest was just as it had been—tall and endless, except now it didn't seem so empty. Some mornings before I fully wake up I can sense a ray of dawn shining hard on my arms or the back of my head, and I'm not surprised that night has departed when I open my eyes. I had a similar feeling now, as if the flat palm of a stare pushed against me.

"Where are you?" I whispered.

I am where I should be.

I turned my head slowly, alert for movement. I noticed how shadow crossed a pebble or a piece of wood, how each object had two colors, two separate levels of brightness that were also somehow the same. I pressed my heels into the ground until I could detect a cool dampness below the dry surface. I slid my gaze steadily over the green lichen that covered one side of a large boulder, and it became as smooth and sleek as mink fur beneath my fingertips. I kept looking as I turned, turning as I looked and looked and looked.

Wait! What was that? A dark gray mitten lay under a raspberry thicket. But no, it wasn't a mitten, it had two shining eyes. It was . . . it was a porcu-

41

pine, and its glare was like sun in my eyes.

"Porcupines can't talk," I reassured myself.

You're a guest in this forest, stupid little boy. Be polite.

"I'm not little, I'm . . ."

That's right. You're big. You've become a man. Now will you go away?

"Are you my guide?" This couldn't be true. I had expected an unusual animal, a dangerous animal, an intelligent animal: a buck with a large rack of antlers. A mountain lion. At the very least, a fox.

No.

I was relieved. "Then why are you talking to me?"

The porcupine was completely still except for her broad, flat nose, which quivered and sampled every scent.

Good question. I'll stop. Good-bye.

"No. Wait. I'm lost." I made my eyes plead for help.

All right. All right. Where do you want to go?

"I can't return home until I learn something new about myself. This is my away time, and I'm supposed get a new name."

How about Lost? That's what you just told me you were.

"Lost is *what* I am, not *who* I am."

Fine. Who are you?

No one had ever asked me such a thing before, and I was annoyed that the porcupine didn't recognize me. "I'm Moss, my father and mother's son."

If you already know, why are you in the woods?

"You don't understand. I'm here to find out more. Who I *really* am. Me."

So, who are you, really, you?

The porcupine's body was tense in her stillness. I knew that if I moved, she would disappear into the raspberries and I'd be alone again. Even though my knees began to ache, even though gnats whined around my ears, I kept very still—but my thoughts raced, searching for an answer. I went back to this morning's conversations in the village with my father and my mother, to my talk with Trouble in the woods, and listened again, listened from outside.

I didn't like what I heard.

"I'm a boy who didn't want guests to come," I said.

Very hospitable.

"I'm a boy who wouldn't help."

How grateful everyone must be to you.

"I'm a boy who's stubborn."

Delightful.

"I'm a boy who broke my grandfather's wampum belt and doesn't have a good story to replace it."

What a pleasure you must be to everyone who knows you.

I thought of my mother, cooking; of my father, having to do all the work for the guests with no son to help him. I thought of Trouble, left alone in the woods. I had never even learned why she had run from the village, never found out why she believed she was a terrible person. I thought of Grandfather, worrying about me.

"I guess I'm not very nice," I said at last. I could find nothing about which to compliment myself.

Good. Now that you know who you are, you can leave me in peace.

The muscles of the porcupine's thick, dark forepaws bunched, and her long claws dug into the earth as if she was preparing to spring away.

"I'm sure this isn't how an away time is supposed to be," I protested. "I haven't learned anything, I haven't become a man."

44

A man, a man, a man, she chided me. *What's a man? You are who you are, and no one but you can tell you the truth about that. Make yourself a man—when you're ready. Don't wait for someone to do it for you.*

✳✳✳

The porcupine closed her eyes, then opened them again. Slowly she straightened her short, stubby legs and padded out from the thicket. As she passed me, she swished her heavy tail, dropping several loose quills. She was in no hurry.

"Don't leave," I said. "Please."

The porcupine paused, sat back on her haunches, sturdy and low to the ground. Angling her head in my direction, she seemed to nod.

"Porcupines can be clever," my mother once told me. She had been constructing a box of birch bark and was thinking of porcupines for decoration. As we talked, she fished with her fingers into a large wooden bowl where quills were soaking in water. When she caught the tip of one with her skin, she studied it for a moment before popping it into her mouth in order to soften it further. She never stuck herself painfully the way I did.

"Porcupines wear their fear on the outside," my

mother went on after she had drawn and flattened the quill through her clamped front teeth and begun to attach it carefully to the top of the box. She was building a design of three wildflowers, her favorite pattern, passed down through her family. "They bother nothing, and nothing bothers them. They allow us the gift of their beauty."

"Beauty?" I laughed. "They don't seem beautiful to me."

My mother raised her eyebrows without looking up. "So, Moss," she asked, "what makes a thing beautiful?"

That kind of question, for which there was no exactly right reply, made me uneasy.

"I don't know," I had said that day.

But now, so close, this porcupine was . . . maybe not beautiful, but certainly she was interesting. Her quills, white with black ends, were a shimmering coat of bristly hair, too many to count. They moved in their own breeze. Her claws were black and polished, and her teeth were orange as a harvest moon. Most surprising was the expression in her eyes. It reminded me of a look Grandfather sometimes gave me when he told me to *think*. It was a look that said, "You already know the answer. Just reach for it." It was a demanding look—not angry or curious—a "Look at that!" look.

After a moment, the porcupine rocked back to all four legs and waddled over to the base of a slippery elm. Using her front paws and lower teeth, she peeled away a strip of bark and began to gnaw at the tender pulp beneath.

I could taste the sweetness—my mother used the same tree to brew a tea. Suddenly I was overcome with a craving so strong I couldn't put it off, so I went to another slippery elm and followed the porcupine's example. The inner pith was soft and chewy, and as the true flavor overtook and overcame the taste I had imagined, I let it fill my mouth with pleasure. Silently, apart and yet together, the porcupine and I shared our meal.

When she was finished the porcupine rubbed her paws together until the pads were clean, and then, lumbering as a fish swimming against a swift current, she pulled herself up the same tree and settled in the crook of a narrow branch. I thought of the fierce animals I had expected to meet during my away time but had not . . . yet, and decided that if I was going to rest, it was safer to be high over the ground than on it. With much greater effort than the porcupine, I climbed my tree as well. Soon I was wedged between a thick limb and the trunk. Leaning forward, I rested my head on the bough.

The forest, from above, was a different place. From where I lay, it was as though I floated on the surface of a clear pond—plants seemed to stretch toward me. Everything was up and down, not sideways—and the world in such straight lines was much neater than it appeared when I was in the middle of it. Below me, paths snaked like grapevines in every direction, leading everywhere, anywhere. Bits of dust floated and glittered in the trees of light that filled the spaces between the trees of wood.

Hugging the bough with my arms, with my whole body, I joined in its stillness. I had fed at its table, I was at rest in its bed. I was the forest's welcomed guest.

CHAPTER FOUR

 I don't know how much time passed. Maybe a little, maybe a lot. When I finally roused myself, I glanced over to the porcupine's tree. Empty. Had she actually spoken to me? Had I dreamed the whole thing?

I swung myself from the branch, hung by my arms, then dropped to the ground and rolled once, cushioned by the blanket of leaves. Instantly I felt a sharp sting in my shoulder, but when I reached around to slap at whatever insect had bitten me, I found instead two long, perfect quills barbed into my skin. Carefully I plucked them out and held them in the palm of my hand. They were straight.

Everywhere you looked from the forest's floor, you saw lines that were round or curved, bent crooked or jagged on the side. You almost never found a stick without a knob, a path without a twist. Most things started out heading one way, then changed, ever so slightly, to go somewhere else. But not quills—and that made them . . . unusual. Beautiful.

I shook my head. Today each new perception seemed important, worth remembering. It was as though there were ideas ready to spring out from whatever I used to believe I knew. No matter where I let my mind roam, I was surprised by what occurred to me.

What was that? Somewhere close by I distinctly heard the sound of two flints clicking together . . . and it was as though a spark lit in me instead of the tinder. I went from being sorry for myself because I was all alone to being afraid for myself because I wasn't. Straining without moving, I tried to learn from my ears everything I wanted to know about this fire that was being started: where it was, who was making it. Soon I heard the crackle of dry wood and smelled the edge of drifting smoke. My arms and legs tightened and I held my breath until, without meaning to, I closed my hand around the quills, sticking myself.

"Ow!"

In reply to my shout, the forest went quiet. Even the trees were waiting for what would happen next.

"You'd better leave me alone," someone called out. "My friends will be back in a minute. A whole hunting party."

The voice was familiar.

"Trouble? Is that you?"

At first there was no answer, and then, "Moss?"

I rushed toward my name, vaulting fallen branches, leaping over rocks, pressing clumps of white violets and trillium deep into the springing ground. "Where are you? I'm coming." As I ran, I saw her. First only the parts that were not concealed by a large oak: the top of her head, her heel, her hands as they pushed dirt to cover a tiny flame. Suddenly, there she was, kneeling, her back to me. Why didn't she turn around?

"What are you doing here?" I asked, breathless, my questions bumping each other. "Were you looking for me? Do you know how to get home? Are you lost, too?"

Why didn't she turn around?

"Leave me alone." Trouble was hunched around herself, her face hidden by her arms. She wouldn't look up.

"What's the matter? Are you hurt?"

Her shoulders gave a shudder, as if she were very cold. It was the kind of movement old people explain by saying that the spirits of children who were never born are calling to them. Then she took a deep breath, unfolded herself, stood up, and faced me. She had changed her clothes and was wearing a breechcloth, leggings, and a short cape—the same as me.

"Why are you dressed like that?" I asked in amazement. "You look like a boy." I laughed at such an idea, but I laughed alone.

Trouble's face was full of anger, and before I could prepare or protect myself, she gave a terrible scream, threw herself at me with a growl, slapping and kicking, knocking me over, kneeling on my arms, pinning them down. She made her hands into clubs, lifted them high over my head. "You followed me," she accused. "You watched."

I struggled to free myself, but Trouble was as strong as I was—and unlike me, she was angry. I had been so happy to see her, so relieved, and now she hated me, wanted to hurt me. Everything was changed, had gone wrong, was bad when it should have been good. I couldn't help myself. Tears filled my eyes, and when I couldn't reach to wipe them away, they ran down the side of my face.

For a moment there was only the battle of our hard breathing, hers sawing at mine, mine pushing at hers, until gradually we both slowed down. Trouble still held her fists above me, but suddenly they seemed to grow heavy and she brought them to her chest. We looked at each other without words. She could tell Shale I had cried, that instead of growing into a man I had turned into a baby, but I didn't care. At least I wasn't still alone.

Trouble got up and lay beside me on the ground. We both stared at the roof of leaves and branches above us.

"Don't cry." Her voice was back to the way it should sound.

I opened my mouth to say "I'm not," but stopped myself. There was no use denying what had happened.

"Don't tell anyone," Trouble said. "Especially Shale."

I propped myself up on one elbow. "Don't tell what?"

But I knew *what* the minute I asked. Trouble was out by herself in the woods, dressed as a boy, her hair arranged like a warrior's, making a fire. It was a story people would think as strange as if I suddenly began to sew a shirt or went to the fields to plant beans.

"I won't," I promised.

She turned her head and studied my eyes, trying to decide whether to believe me. When I didn't look away, her expression lost some of its storminess—but still we watched each other, waiting for understanding. Finally Trouble broke the silence.

"When I met you before," she said, "and you told me you were going for your away time, at first I thought you were just blowing air, that you would back down and go home. But then, when you actually left, it made me decide: if you could do something so . . . *yourself*, so could I."

I didn't tell her the truth: that I had come to the forest for the wrong reasons. That I had come because my parents had not stopped me, as I had hoped they would. That I had come because I refused to be hospitable. That I had come because I was a child, not because I was brave—like her.

"I told you I had an argument with my mother and sisters," Trouble went on. "Then my father came home . . . "

I nodded, nodded again for her to continue. In response, Trouble turned away to stare into the trees.

"They're always at me," she said after a moment. "Teasing me that I'm more boy than girl, telling me that nobody will ever want me for a wife."

"A *wife*?" I laughed, trying to imagine Trouble as a grown-up woman, like my mother.

Trouble's whole body whipped around to face me. She was furious again, and lashed out. "You think that's funny? You crybaby."

The insult brought back Grandmother's joke about my name and mixed it with the shame of what had just happened. I was so unprepared for the return of Trouble's anger, for its slap, that I could not defend myself against it. My cheeks blazed and . . . I hung my head away before she could see my eyes.

"I'm sorry." Trouble touched my arm with her fingertips. "You see? My father's right. I am a terrible person."

"You're not terrible." "Terrible" was too important a thing for people like us to be.

"Different, then. A disappointment." Like "terrible," she said "disappointment" as if repeating someone else's accusation.

"You don't like being a girl?"

"Would *you* want to be one?"

The idea had never come to me before. If I had been asked that question anytime before today, I probably would have stuck out my tongue, covered my ears. Now, however, nothing seemed too impossible to at least consider. When I tried to picture my life as a girl, it was as though once more I was up on that high bough, looking down at a familiar scene but seeing it in a new way. And here's what I realized: I didn't understand enough about being a girl to know what I thought.

"I'm not sure," I confessed to Trouble honestly. I took a long breath, raised my eyes to hers. "Tell me about being a girl before I answer."

She looked doubtful that I was serious but began anyway.

"There are all these things you're not allowed to do."

"Such as?"

"Sleep outside. Hunt with your uncle. Go places with boys outside your clan."

"I can't go places with girls outside *my* clan," I reminded her. I didn't like to allow that someone else had more to complain about than I did.

"Yes, but you don't want to, so it doesn't seem as though it's forbidden," Trouble said.

I had no fast answer to that. She was right. And yet . . .

"But," I thought out loud, "*we're* here together."

Trouble blinked, opened her mouth, closed it again.

Now that we remembered we were breaking a rule, Trouble and I became shy of each other. We sat up straighter, moved farther apart.

"What's so good about being a boy, anyway?" I said. "Everyone is always telling you how to act, what you're doing wrong, how you'll never grow up to be the right kind of man."

Trouble looked at me. She was not convinced.

"Girls have it easier," I went on. "No one expects you to do anything."

"*What?*" Trouble opened her eyes wide and leaned so far toward me that I shrank back.

"Well, they don't," I argued. "You get to stay warm at home and wait for the meat to appear. There's nothing you have to do, like learn to use a bow or risk your life to protect everyone else if some enemies attack us. And then when you get old, you get to boss all your relatives around."

Trouble picked up a rock that was lying on the ground next to her and threw it so hard at a tree that it bounced off, just missing me.

"*Get* to stay home?" she demanded? "*You* stay home. *You* work in the cornfields all summer. *You* try to sew deerskin. *You* listen to all the stories about hunting or going to new places and never see them for yourself. *You* have your mother and your aunts and your grandmother—especially your grand-mother—watch you all the time and never be proud. *You* feel like you never understand the why of anything!"

"I *don't*," I yelled back. "And no one ever explains it, either."

"They just tell you to wait, to 'be patient,' to not ask so many questions. And if you do, you're 'diffi-cult,' 'not the way you used to be.' 'Terrible.'"

"They smile at you as though you're a dumb lit-tle kid. 'Just do what we say.'"

"'Don't argue.'"

"'Don't upset your mother.'"

"'Don't make your father angry.'"

"'Don't disappoint your grandfather.'"

"What about what *I* want?" we both said at exactly the same time. Our words seemed to flow together, then ricocheted off the trees like Trouble's rock until they fell back upon us. When they did, I

59

stared at the ground very hard for a moment, then sneaked a glance at Trouble, who was doing the same to me. Her shoulders were hunched and her lips were pulled wide across her teeth. From somewhere deep inside me, a laugh got started and fought its way up through my nose. Trouble clapped both hands over her mouth, but it was too late and she gave a loud groan as she tried to hold her own laugh inside her body. That was too much for me. I let down all the barriers against how funny we sounded, how funny she looked because now she was pointing at me with both hands, shaking her head no, no, no.

"Poor. Moss." Trouble was giggling so much that her words burst like seeds popping from a pod.

I fell over on my back, kicked my heels against the ground, twisted over onto my stomach, and pressed my face against the dry leaves. Still my laughter kept coming, like bubbles shooting to the surface of water. Each time that I almost stopped, I would hear Trouble, who was laughing in a voice so low that she could have been a frog. A FROG! Suddenly a frog seemed the craziest animal in the world and I couldn't help laughing at the idea of it, all green and homely, so earnest about itself, croaking and hopping. HOPPING! Hopping was surely the silliest way of moving I could think of.

"A frog!" I called to Trouble, and looked up. She nodded, shook her head, nodded again. She couldn't speak but, incredibly, she understood. She pointed to her throat. She knew what she sounded like and that only made her laugh lower, which made her sound even *more* like a frog. That made me laugh so hard I made a squeaking noise—which was even funnier than a frog croak, or at least Trouble seemed to think so because she imitated it once as she caught her breath and . . . that *really* was funny. We started croaking and squeaking back and forth to each other, like a new language that only we could talk, a language as weird as the one that the guests spoke.

"Aye," I said, imitating them. "Nay."

I got dizzy from laughing, lost my breath from laughing. My stomach hurt from laughing. Tears ran from my eyes. Everything was funny. A fly landed on my nose. A FLY LANDED ON MY NOSE!

I threw my laughing to the sky like bunches of

grapes and, little by little, each one got smaller than the last, each one sailed less high into the air than the one before, until eventually I wasn't laughing anymore, just humming under my breath, sighing like a sleeping puppy. I wiped my eyes and turned my head to see what Trouble was doing.

Usually, if by accident I found myself staring directly into someone else's eyes, I would quickly glance away, pretending that the contact had never happened. Usually if someone seemed too close, I would run. Usually if a girl smiled at me, I would laugh or blush or get confused. But not this time. This time, I smiled back.

CHAPTER FIVE

 "What have you got in your hand?" Trouble asked.

The two quills were still pressed against my palm, light as air.

"Nothing," I said. If I showed her, she'd ask how I found them, and I didn't know what to say about the porcupine. She wouldn't understand the talking part—how I had been forced to listen to my own voice.

"Did you make a fire?" I inquired, to change the subject.

Trouble's curiosity did not disappear. "Show me," she insisted.

Quills would have been an easy thing to explain. I could have said I had found them on the ground, which was true enough. I could have made a joke, told her about being stuck, then thrown the quills away. But I didn't want to do that. Somehow the whole story of the porcupine was too private, too . . . mysterious . . . to use up that way. So instead, I imitated the porcupine. I frowned at Trouble in a serious manner and shoved her wondering back at her.

"I still don't understand," I said. "What are you doing out here today? What are you thinking? What do you want?"

Trouble's face became thoughtful. At first she didn't answer and waited for me to go on. Yet I could tell there was something on her mind, something she cared about more than knowing what I held in my hand, something that was too difficult not to tell.

"You're really asking me?"

Now I was the one who was curious.

"Oh yes," I assured her, and slipped the quills into my pouch. To my surprise, I really was interested in her story.

"All right, then," Trouble decided. "Did you ever hear about my grandmother Boulder's sister? About Running Woman?"

The name sounded familiar.

"Didn't she have to leave?" I remembered. "Didn't she go far away and . . . ?" I had overheard my mother talking about Running Woman with some of her friends, but I couldn't recall much of what they said. Instead, I remembered how they sounded when they spoke of her. Whispering. Pleased to be shocked. Happy in a way that wasn't familar to me.

Trouble's eyes were very bright. "I'm like her."

"How? Remind me of what she did." I rested my head on my arm, closed my eyes so that I could follow the words without distraction, and waited through that little space of quiet that always separates a story from ordinary events.

"It happened a long time ago," Trouble began.

✶✶✶

RUNNING WOMAN

When Running Woman was a little girl everyone worried about her. Even as a baby, she didn't sleep much. Her legs appeared to be too long, her hands too big, and she was not beautiful. Even worse, she was difficult for her parents to manage, which is why she was called Mistake.

As Mistake grew older, she did not grow easier. When she met other children she forced them to obey her. In games of tag, she always had to be "it," deciding whom to catch first; in dodgeball, she avoided being hit so well that the other team got tired of trying. When she and her cousins played house, she insisted on being the grand-mother so that she could tell everyone else how to act. Mistake was so convinced of her own importance and value that it was impossible to disagree with her, so sure of her opinions that no one could persuade her to change her mind and see a situation in another way. Worst of all, most of the time she was right about what she believed, so she never learned a lesson from an error, never was shown up to be foolish, never had to apologize after being proven wrong.

Mistake, people had to admit, was good at every task she tried. Too good, some believed. What will happen, they worried, when she meets another person who is stronger or smarter or even more confident than she is?

No one was more concerned about this problem than Bridgemaker, Mistake's father, for he truly loved his daughter and secretly was pleased whenever Mistake had another success. He shook his head and sighed if his brother-in-law or hunting partners came to him with reports of yet another incident—like the morning that Mistake jumped into a lake from a branch higher than anyone else or the afternoon that she held her breath underwater longer than her older cousins or the night, by the fire, when she won a contest of not blinking with Find-the-Bear, the strongest man in the village.

"What will become of her?" Bridgemaker complained aloud, but then, when he repeated the stories about their daughter to his wife, Starlight, he pinched his nose to keep from laughing and whispered, "Find-the-Bear has met his match!"

Starlight was less certain that Mistake should be encouraged. "What if she had made him angry?" she asked her husband. "What if she accepts too risky a dare? What if she is never content with performing ordinary work, jobs that no one talks about but everyone depends upon? Planting? Grinding cornmeal? Repairing tools? Carrying water?"

Starlight had reason to be troubled: once Mistake had demonstrated that she was the best at an activity, she had no wish to do it again. She preferred the new over the old, the exciting over the safe, the quick over the slow. By the time she had reached the age where she was ready to change from being a girl to being a woman, there seemed to her almost nothing left to do for the first time.

"You must settle down, now," Starlight advised. "You must master many ordinary jobs so that you will be responsible, dependable, steady, and strong. It's a woman's way to be so skilled at her work that it becomes invisible. It is a woman's way to hold the world together by the force of her quietness."

"Not me." Mistake could barely stand to sit still long enough to listen to her mother's words.

"Well," Starlight went on, "there are girls who go the other way and take on the jobs of a man. It's an honorable choice. Is that what you plan for yourself? To leave home every day in search of food? To spend your evenings unbending wood to make arrows and bows? To prepare the fields for planting instead of harvesting them?"

To Mistake, however, a man's life sounded just as boring as a woman's. "Not me," she said.

"What, then?" Starlight threw up her hands. "You

can't keep yourself from growing up."

"Yes, I can," Mistake promised, and wondered how.

✳✳✳

One summer night soon after that, Mistake and her younger sister—who at the time was called Blackberry—were bathing in a stream that led from the village to the sea. The breeze was warm against their skin, drying them quickly each time they stood up. The full moon was the color of the foam left by waves on the beach, and small brown bats danced in the sky. Everything was as it should be, and yet Mistake was not happy. She remained still for such a long time that her feet sank into the mud of the bank.

"Tell me to do something unusual," she said to Blackberry.

"Like what?"

"I don't care. Anything, as long as it's a surprise to me."

"Make a boat out of a leaf," Blackberry suggested helpfully. "Then we can watch it sail away."

"There's no leaf big enough to carry me," Mistake said.

"Blow on a dandelion ball," Blackberry offered. "Then we can watch the wings float into the dark."

"I am too heavy to be lifted by them," Mistake said.

"Dig a deep hole," Blackberry proposed. "Maybe you'll find some clamshells."

"I am already in a deep enough hole," Mistake said.

Blackberry rarely understood all the words exactly when her older sister was in such a mood, but she thought Mistake was so perfect and wonderful that she never admitted her confusion. All she desired was for Mistake to smile at her, and so she kept searching for a good plan. A sudden gust of wind sent a ripple across the water.

"I know." Blackberry clapped her hands because she was certain Mistake would like what she was about to say. "Why don't you race the wind?"

Mistake opened her mouth, but no words came. She raised her chin, stretched her neck, and in the pale light Blackberry could see her sister's eyes flash.

"To where?"

"To wherever it goes," Blackberry answered quickly and without thinking. She was glad Mistake had not found a reason to dismiss her idea.

"I love you," Mistake said. Then, with wet, plopping sounds, she pulled first one foot and then the other free from where they had been stuck. "I'll be back when I win," she called, and before Blackberry could realize what was *happening, Mistake was off, running toward the beach, then along it so fast that the wind could not overtake her, even to comb her long hair back from her shoulders. Her bare feet thudded on the ground, loudly as she started and then more and more softly as she got farther away.*

"No!" Blackberry cried, but her voice was too slow. The wind trailed Mistake like the wake of water that chases a swift canoe. Blackberry felt the drag, the pull of her sister's escape. Its power frightened her so badly that she pressed her body against a large rock, clutched at it with her fingers, so that she too would not be yanked into the ebbing tide.

✳✳✳

"Boulder was my grandmother, but I'm much more like Running Woman," Trouble said to bring us back.

"Did she ever return home?" I asked, still held by the story.

"People say they have seen her before a gusty night. They tell her to go away quickly so that she won't lead storms to the village. The wind is so angry that it can't overtake her that it blows away everything wherever she leads it."

"Then it seems to me that if she truly cared about

71

the village, she would stop—let the wind catch her —so that it wouldn't take revenge on other people. She made a selfish choice."

Trouble became alert, as if ready to contradict me. Several times she started to speak but was stopped by arguments inside her own mind. Finally she simply shook her head sharply.

"If everybody ran away, there'd be no village," I went on. "If Boulder had followed her sister, there'd be no you."

Trouble scowled at me. She didn't like to hear criticism of Running Woman.

"What happened to your grandmother after that night?"

Trouble thought for a moment. "She went back to her parents and told them that Mistake was gone. Bridgemaker and Starlight and all their relatives searched until dawn and through the next day. They thought that if they called for Mistake, their oldest daughter might be insulted and would never return. That's where the name Running Woman came from."

"Did they ever find her?"

"No. For a long time they blamed Blackberry for not convincing her sister to stay. People started to call her Boulder as a kind of joke, and for a while my grandmother hated that name—it reminded her of what she hadn't done. But then she changed her mind."

"Why?" I thought of Boulder, who was large and heavy, the first old woman people consulted when they wanted sound advice. She made visitors feel welcome, even children who weren't members of her clan.

"It was because of my grandfather, Sun-in-His-Eyes. My grandmother told me that Boulder, in his voice, became a strong word."

"Wouldn't it make Boulder sad if now you ran away, too, like her sister?"

Trouble thought about my question, considered it from every angle the way she might study a rock in a stream before putting her full weight upon it. As I watched, her body seemed to change, to drop some of its guard, to relax . . . and then to become tense again.

"Boulder won't even . . . ," Trouble said, then

stopped herself. "I don't care," she said.

But she did.

✳✳✳

We stood up, brushed ourselves off, and looked around. Trouble glanced at my belt, and I realized that she had not forgotten the quills in my pouch.

"How was the feast?" I asked, to divert her. "Did the guests make any mistakes? Did they at least remember to bring something to eat with?" The last time one of them had visited, the man hadn't even observed that simplest, everyday duty. My father had to pretend not to be hungry and lend out his own bowl and spoon.

Trouble gave me a strange look. "How should I know? The guests hadn't arrived yet when I went back to the village."

I rested my forehead against the smooth white bark of a birch tree. It hardly seemed possible that so little time had passed for other people since this morning. Usually, I didn't measure the passage of a day, except by meals and light. If the sun was dim and getting brighter—and we ate corn mush—it was morning. If the sun was bright and getting dimmer—and we ate meat or fish—it was evening. In

74

between was berry time, honey time. If my stomach was still full, the hour was early. If my stomach demanded to be refilled, it was getting late. But, in the shadow of high trees, in the absence of the smell of any food, I had lost my counting stick.

And there was something else: most ordinary days I didn't have many new ideas. I did the same things, went to the same places, said the same words to the same people. But in the woods, away from everything familiar, my thoughts had accumulated like fresh drifts after a blizzard. Today . . . today time inside my mind moved faster than time outside it.

Wait! Even now my thoughts were outdistancing my reach. I could pause to let the afternoon catch up to where I had arrived. Mother and Father had not yet missed me, were not yet worried. Probably they still hoped that I would reconsider, come back, help them with the guests. And I could! I would!

"Do you know the way home?" I asked Trouble.

"Of course." She shrugged, gestured to the left with her chin. "It's not far at all."

CHAPTER SIX

 I had never returned home before today, because before today I had never truly left it.

Home was the place I never saw because I saw it all the time, too up close to see it well. Home was me and I was home—there was no space between us. "Not home" was too big to think about, too far away to reach. "Not home" was where strangers lived, where monsters roamed, where lost people found themselves when they disappeared. "Not home" was the last spot a person would want to stay, no matter how interesting or exciting it might seem for a while. And now "not home" was where I was glad to leave.

As we approached, I heard home before I saw it: the rustle of voices, the rat-a-tat of laughter, the bang of wood being chopped. I sensed the wide echo of a space cleared of trees and felt the earth vibrate in a packed thatch of many footsteps going and coming. I smelled . . . food! Turkey and roasting corn, a rich blanket of bean soup, every good thing there was to eat. Each step brought me closer to the swirl of colors that flashed in the narrow bands between tree trunks, and it was all I could do not to burst into the village like a rain squall, touching and grabbing each person I passed.

But when I looked over at Trouble, I could tell that for her this return was not easy, not a victory. Her skin was dark and flushed, as if she had been running too fast, and her eyes were hard. At first I didn't understand what was bothering her, and then I did: she was still dressed as a boy. Certainly people would notice, laugh, throw questions she didn't want to catch.

"Where are your other clothes?" I asked her casually, not wanting to embarrass her further. "Your skirt?"

She shook her head. "I left it at my house. I was in a hurry and, anyway, I didn't plan to wear it again. I thought . . . I would be changed."

I nodded. Trouble had been like me, thinking change was something magic, something that happened fast. But change took more than putting on different clothes or finding a porcupine willing to talk. This afternoon we were still who we had been this morning, just perhaps a little more so.

"You stay here," I said. "I'll go to your house and bring you something to put on. Then people won't have to know what you did unless you want to tell them."

At first I thought Trouble was angry. Her cheeks got as tight as if she were sucking cranberries, and her eyebrows pulled close together. But then her face cleared. "You surprise me."

"Wait for me," I said.

After I had taken a few steps, I looked over my

shoulder. Trouble seemed very alone, even more than when she was by herself in the woods. There was something else that needed to happen between us. I came back to where she stood, reached into the pouch at my waist, and showed her what she had wanted to see.

Trouble looked at the two quills, then at me.

"Take one," I offered. "To keep you company."

She reached carefully, gently, into my flat palm. She of course saw quills every day, just as I did, but she sensed these were special. She picked the nearest one, held it for a moment between her thumb and her forefinger before tucking it deep into the dark coil of her hair.

✳✳✳

Naturally, the first person who saw me had to be Shale.

"Moss!" he called so loudly that everyone around us turned to look. "Where have you been? Who were you with? Where did you go? What did you do?"

There was only one way to deal with Shale, and that was to turn his questions back on him.

"Where have *you* been, Shale?" I demanded.

"I've searched everywhere for you. I was afraid you were sick from eating a spider—and were hiding."

"A spider?! Hiding?!" Shale was shocked at this thought about himself and interested in finding out more about it, as I knew he would be. "Why would I be hiding? Where would I hide? Where did you search?"

"*You* know," I said, as if he and I shared a secret. That made all the listeners pay attention.

"I do?"

"I don't want to say too much," I added.

"Thank you!" Shale forgot that he had no idea what I was talking about.

"Now I must go tell them I've found you," I said, and rushed past him.

"Yes," Shale agreed before he caught himself. "Tell *who*?" he called behind me, but too late.

Almost everyone in the village was assembled in the clearing that ran between the two sets of houses, so I ran behind the nearest row to avoid seeing anyone else. As I passed between the low bark buildings, I noticed that the guests had arrived. They were sitting on the ground, clustered in a little group as if waiting to be told what to do, and they wore so many clothes! They looked . . . like food shut up too long in a tight-lidded box.

I watched for my father, my mother, not sure what I would say if I saw them. Like Shale, they would wonder about what had happened to me but they wouldn't ask. They'd wait until I told them.

Trouble's house was empty and I ducked through the doorway. The girls' sleeping mats were on the ground to the left, all neatly settled and arranged . . . except for one that was rumpled, with a deerskin skirt tossed in a heap. I snatched it up, rolled it into a ball, and rushed outside again—only to crash into Trouble's sister Eggshell. She was younger than I, but old enough to be curious.

"What have you got, Moss?" she asked.

"Nothing."

Eggshell was as short as Trouble was tall. Standing in front of me, blocking my way, her eyes were directly at the level of my chest. She studied the bundle I clutched.

"Nothing," I repeated.

Eggshell's expression suddenly lit up with pleasure. "She's back, isn't she?" she whispered to me. "She came back. She came back."

"I don't know . . . ," I searched for some excuse.

"I was scared," Eggshell said. "I thought she'd be like Running Woman—she talks about her all the time—and it would be my fault because I teased her too much."

Eggshell was so relieved, I couldn't lie to her.

"Trouble's fine," I told her. "She asked me to get her dress. I'm taking it to her now."

"Let me come, too. Please, Moss," Eggshell begged. "I won't tell anyone."

What would Trouble think if I brought Eggshell along? She said she had fought with her sisters, but Eggshell seemed very anxious to see her. . . .

"All right, then."

"Yes!" Eggshell clapped her hands together. "Wait, though." She ran back into the house and a moment later emerged holding a belt decorated with shells. "Tonight is a feast," she explained. "Trouble can't arrive in just her usual dress, as if this were an ordinary meal. What would the guests think?"

The guests again. They were the cause of all of

this, of every strange and confusing thing that had happened to me today.

✳✳✳

"Moss?"

I was almost out of the village. I recognized Cloud's voice and shot a quick look to Eggshell, who pressed her lips together to show she remembered her promise.

"I'll meet you at my house," I told Cloud.

"Where are you going?" He looked at Eggshell as if to ask, *What are you doing with her?* "What are you hiding under your arm?"

He was as bad as Shale but could not be discouraged so easily.

"I've been out in the woods," I said softly, and then, after a beat of silence, I added, "alone."

"Alone?" Cloud was surprised. He could not seem to puzzle out the meaning of my words. "Look, Moss. Just because there were things about away time that I couldn't explain to you yet . . ."

"Now you don't have to." I closed my eyes slowly, then opened them.

"It's not that I don't want to," Cloud continued as

83

if he hadn't heard me. "It's just that . . . you have to be older to understand."

"I am older," I answered.

"No, I mean, you have to have been out in the woods . . ." His voice trailed off. At last he realized what I had just told him.

"Alone," I repeated.

"You went?" He couldn't believe it. "Today? Already? So fast? At this time of year?"

I scratched my leg, ignoring his questions.

"What happened?" he finally wanted to know.

"I'm sorry," I said. "I can't explain it. It was very . . . private." I thought of the porcupine. If she heard me sounding so proud of myself she would probably bite my foot.

Cloud was still amazed. "You really went? Really?"

I shrugged. "Doesn't everyone?"

He suddenly remembered Eggshell and looked at her. "Why are you with her?"

"That's private, too," I answered quickly. If only he would go away.

"If you actually did your away time then you

must have a new name," Cloud insisted. He was very bothered by my announcement. It was as though I had taken something from him before he was ready to give it.

Cloud knew as well as I did that a new name didn't always come right away. Sometimes a person had to figure out what had happened to him first. Still, there was no denying it—I hadn't gotten a name. Did that mean my away time wasn't good enough? "Lost" is what the porcupine had called me, but that didn't sound very impressive. How could I answer Cloud? I had said, "It's private" too many times already.

"What is it, then?" Cloud smiled as though he had hopes of getting back that thing he was afraid I had taken too soon.

"Thunder," a deep voice rumbled from the forest behind where we stood. I was so startled that I jumped—but Cloud was even more surprised and didn't notice. The only person who seemed calm was Eggshell, who broke into a wide grin. Two of her front teeth were missing and the new ones hadn't yet grown in to fill the empty space.

"That's right," she said. "Moss is Thunder now. But don't tell," she warned Cloud.

He looked from Eggshell to the trees, from the trees to Eggshell, then to the trees again, then back at me. What else could I do? I nodded.

"I don't know what's going on," Cloud said nervously, "but I'm late for the feast. We'll talk about all this later on." And with one last, uneasy glance toward the woods, he turned around and walked into the village.

Now it was my turn to stare at Eggshell. "What was that?" I whispered to her.

"Only me, *Thunder*," said Trouble, and stepped out from behind an oak tree.

✳✳✳

Trouble put on her skirt and belt, and Eggshell helped braid her hair into two long plaits while I went to the stream to wash my face. I would have to deal with Cloud soon, and he would expect some explanation for what had just taken place. I couldn't pretend to have a name that wasn't mine—which was too bad, because I liked Thunder quite a bit. It was just the kind of serious name I wanted for myself.

On the way into the village, we met my father, coming toward us. He had been running, but he slowed down to a walk and tried to act casual.

"Cloud said you were over this way," he said between short breaths. "Your mother and I were wondering when to expect you at home."

His eyes were tired. I had been missed, no doubt of it, but that thought did not bring me any satisfaction. In my mind when I left was the idea that I would make my parents regret not paying more attention to my opinion. "They'll wish they had treated me better when I'm not around" was what I had told myself—and somehow now I knew that was exactly what had happened. I had listened to my mother and father talking to each other so many times that I could almost hear the words they would have used, first my father blaming himself, then my mother blaming herself, to make him feel better.

But when I looked at my father's face, the only person *I* could blame was me. On a day when he already had much to do, I had added worry. And, quite unexpectedly, I realized something so obviously true that I couldn't believe I hadn't seen it all along: my father didn't want the guests to come any more than I did. He liked our family time, too. He didn't need the extra work. He felt uncomfortable around strangers—he just wasn't permitted to show it. I could run away because I was still a boy, but he, a man, had to stay, had to do what was obliged of him, had to obey rules, even more than I did . . . because if he didn't, he'd be wrong in his own eyes.

I didn't know how to say to him all the things I felt, and that made me feel them all the stronger. Because they couldn't get out, I had to make them a part of me—the way once you learn to swim, that's a part of you, or once you learn to like the first snow-fall of winter.

"Your mother keeps using up all the dry wood in her cooking fire," my father said quietly.

He wasn't telling me what to do, wasn't shaming me, just giving me a choice if I wanted to make it. I looked back to the stream and the forest beyond it.

"There's plenty more just over there," I said. "I'll bring an armload as I come."

He nodded. "Good idea." There were things he felt that he couldn't show, too, but I knew he approved. "I'll do the same."

"We should bring some home, too," Eggshell said to Trouble. "As long as we're here."

Trouble rolled her eyes. Going back was still not easy, but she didn't argue, and together the four of us went into the brush, loaded ourselves down with sticks and branches piled almost higher than our eyes, and walked that way into the wide clearing where people from all over the village had assembled. We passed the fires of many families, passed the guests, still seated alone and hunched together. When we came to our house, my father and I stopped and dropped our wood by the side of the doorway.

My mother, hearing the sound, came outside wiping her hands on a leafy stick. When she saw me she seemed ready to speak, but then she met my father's eyes, changed her mind, and waited.

"Moss was in the forest gathering wood for our meal," my father said.

My mother pursed her lips, smiled at him, and touched my head. "How fortunate."

CHAPTER SEVEN

 Grandfather had seated himself near the guests but paid no attention to them. His arms were crossed tightly over his chest and his legs were folded beneath his body in such a way that he could get up quickly if he needed to. He stared straight ahead and held his face stern, as if his ideas had led him very far away.

"Why is Grandfather upset?" I asked my father.

"The strangers brought no gifts to the village," he answered. "Your grandfather decided that if they could not be proper guests, he didn't have to be a proper host."

"What will they make of his rudeness?" my mother asked my father.

"They'll think he is an old man," my father answered. "Surely there are old men among them, too, just as difficult."

"Someone should say *something*." Too much silence made my mother nervous. "It's not polite for people to be next to each other for too long without words to connect them. Go." She gestured to my father with a tilt of her chin. "You were the one who invited them. Tell them a story while I finish the meal."

My father was not happy at this idea.

"They won't understand what he says," I reminded her, looking over at the guests.

"It doesn't matter," my mother insisted. "They must have tales of their own, so they'll recognize that it's a story from the way you tell it. It will put them at ease."

"Which story, then?"

As she thought about my father's question, turning possibilities over in her head, my mother bent to pick up some of my wood and tuck it into the fire. The soup was bubbling, and even the smoke smelled wonderful.

"Tell them . . . tell them . . . I know: tell them about how human beings got separated from each other."

Father glanced at me, helpless. This was a story everyone knew, a story that was offered to guests to make them feel as if they weren't truly strangers but simply cousins from another clan who had come at last to visit their relatives.

"My father could tell it better," my father protested.

"He could," my mother agreed. "But he won't."

We all turned to watch Grandfather, who kept himself so stiff that he could have been a pine stump.

"All right, then." Father began to walk toward the group. "Don't say I never follow your suggestions. Come on, Moss. You can at least accompany me."

✳✳✳

When the guests saw us approaching they shifted their legs and seemed to huddle even closer together. They watched Father's movements carefully, the way nesting seagulls regard a human being who walks along the beach. They seemed distrustful, embarrassed at their odd clothes and strange hair, and as I observed them, yet another new thought came to me: the guests were no happier being guests than we were being hosts! They looked as though they'd rather be anywhere else but where they were. It could not have been easy for them to be surrounded by people they didn't understand, who said so little, who treated them properly out of habit, not out of friendship or the likelihood of having a good time. For all they knew, Father, who frowned to himself in annoyance, could have been angry with them.

We sat at the edge of their ragged circle, and my father spoke first to Grandfather.

"Your daughter-in-law thinks we should entertain them with the tale of how human beings got separated from each other." He waited, hoping that Grandfather would take over. When Grandfather pretended not to hear, my father sighed, adjusted his body so that he was opposite the guests. He patted the ground for me to sit beside him, then he opened his hands on his knees to indicate that he was about to tell a story—and began.

***

HOW THE PEOPLE LOST EACH OTHER

A long time ago, all human beings were part of the same tribe. There were so many people that their village was too large to remain for more than a year in any one spot, because all the food in the area would be eaten up: the animals would be hunted, the corn harvested, the water drunk, the berries picked. When this happened, it was necessary for people to pack every possession, every hoe and lance, every bowl and spoon and sleeping mat, every mask, every grinding stone, and begin a journey to find a new place to live.

This trip was especially hard for the very old and the very young, who would have soon fallen behind the rest except for a clever plan: a small number of healthy and strong men and women went first in the procession. Their tasks were to find new lands, to warn those who came after if there was any danger to be avoided, to locate good sites for temporary camps, and to break a path that was easy to walk.

All the rest of the healthy and strong men and women came last. Their jobs were to make sure that the ground over which people passed was left clean, that the animals who lived there were thanked, and to protect the rear.

Between these two groups traveled the grandmothers and grandfathers and the small children. Their jobs were to be safe, to tell stories, to laugh and to sing, to remember the old days and to prepare for the new ones. They neither had to go too fast—those before them had that responsibility—nor worry if they went too slowly, for those behind them were in no hurry. There was only one strict law they were instructed to follow: they must not touch or disturb anything along the way unless it was absolutely necessary. This was out of respect for those parts of the earth that were not destined to become a home for human beings.

Now it happened that on one of these great journeys there was a grandmother who loved her granddaughter too much. The grandmother, whose name was Can't Say No, believed that her granddaughter, whose name was Never Enough, could do nothing wrong. The old lady indulged the child's every whim, comforted her every cry. If the dried meat was tough, Can't Say No chewed it first and then gave it, softened, to Never Enough. If the ground was rocky, Can't Say No insisted that Never Enough sleep atop her stomach. If the wind was cold or wet, Can't Say No let Never Enough walk within the shelter of her wide skirt.

But no matter how many kindnesses Can't Say No bestowed on Never Enough, Never Enough always wanted more. If Can't Say No found two ripe plums hanging from a branch, Never Enough asked for both of them. If Can't Say No sang three songs to lull her granddaughter to sleep, Never Enough demanded three more. If Can't Say No carried Never Enough up a hill to spare her young legs, Never Enough begged to be carried down the hill as well. But Can't Say No dearly loved the little girl and didn't complain, even to the other old ladies, who disapproved of such indulgence.

On a warm afternoon in early spring, the men and women at the head of the group came upon a broad frozen river and debated among themselves what was to be done. Some believed that the ice was solid, and proposed that everyone walk across to the other bank—which appeared to be a fine place to construct the next village. Others were not so confident, suggesting that the people should follow the river upstream until it became more narrow or more shallow, and make the crossing there. After much conversation, after testing and tapping the crust with poles, it was decided that it was safe enough to walk on the river as long as the passage was made quickly, a few people at a time, with no stopping along the way.

And so the first group of men and women, one by one or two by two, stepped lightly to the other side and, indeed, they experienced no problems of any sort. In fact, there was only one unusual thing about the trip: halfway between the two banks, a beautifully shaped deer antler stuck out from the ice, as if the buck to whom it belonged had been caught beneath the river's waves in the sudden sweep of winter. Everyone who saw the horn remarked on it, so graceful were its curves and arches, and many took its presence as good luck, a sign that soon a new home would be found.

When all the men and women in the first group were on the opposite side, the turn came for the elderly and the children. Exactly midway through that group, Can't Say No, who of course carried Never Enough on her back, tiptoed onto the ice. The surface hummed with the power of rushing water, which could be glimpsed as a dull gleam far below. The air was heavy with the promise of spring-time, and Can't Say No hurried to join those who had pre-ceded her.

"Wait!" commanded Never Enough at the center of the river and pointed at the horn. "I want to see."

Can't Say No paused, even bent low so that Never Enough would have a better view.

"I want to touch it!" Never Enough climbed down from her grandmother and ran over to within an arm's reach of the antler's tip.

"I want to take it with me," Never Enough announced, and grabbed one slender point in her fist. Can't Say No remembered all the instructions—how nothing was supposed to be disturbed, especially on this particular part of the journey—but Never Enough's eyes were shining with desire and she couldn't bear to disap-point the little girl.

"Take it, then, but quickly, before anyone notices," Can't Say No whispered, and with that, Never Enough tugged with all her strength.

A moan arose from the ice, followed by the creak of a

racing crack that instantly stretched in a ragged line from either side of the horn to each distant bank. It all took place so quickly that no one had time to cry out a warning or to be afraid, and with each passing second the space dividing the ice widened and was filled with a flood of roily waves.

On one side stood Never Enough, still clutching the horn, and on the other, Can't Say No, who lifted her arms and called to her granddaughter, "Let go. Leap to me."

"It's too far," cried Never Enough, who didn't want to abandon the horn. "You come here."

And Can't Say No, who moved faster than she had moved in many years, flung herself across the chasm. She fell heavily next to the child, so heavily that the ice all around them broke away, creating a frozen pale island big enough for just the two of them.

As everyone else watched from the two shores, the awakened river pushed the island downstream, and the last sight anyone saw of Can't Say No and Never Enough was of the two of them, their bodies pressed close against each other, heading toward the sea.

✳ ✳ ✳

"The people who had already crossed the river went on to create a new tribe," my father finished the story. "They were our ancestors. And the people who had not yet crossed went on to form all the others. Even yours." He gestured to the guests pleasantly, as was the welcoming-back custom.

"Unless these are the children of Never Enough," muttered Grandfather, but of course only we understood him.

"It's time to eat," Mother called. "Come inside before the storm."

I had been so absorbed in my father's story that I hadn't paid attention to the rising wind, to the dark clouds that had rolled overhead to block the late afternoon sun, to the invisible bits of snow that filled the air, mixed with cold rain, and stung my skin. The guests seemed to notice the weather for the first time also. They might not have understood Father's words, but they had been held by the rhythm of his voice, the flash of his eyes, the clap of his hands when the ice cracked in two.

Now everyone crowded together under the cover of bark roofs, filling houses with sound and the conversations of people relieved not to be wet. As the approaching gale howled and roared outside, I couldn't help wondering how Trouble had been received by her family. Had they asked her too closely about where she had been all afternoon? Had Eggshell kept her promise?

It was as if my thoughts had summoned her. Suddenly Trouble raced past our doorway, her hair wild and braided only on one side.

"I'll be back," I said to my mother, who was handing me a bowl of soup.

"Where . . . ?" she cried, her voice full of all the worry she had hidden earlier, but I had no time to answer. I ran in the direction Trouble had taken, calling her name, calling Trouble to come back, calling Trouble to wait for me.

There! I saw her splash across the creek, the wind whipping her dress against the back of her legs and shoulders, and I followed, gained on her in my determination. Finally I was close enough to grab her arm.

"Let go," she shouted above the noise of bending branches, and tried to shake free. Leaves spun around us like a school of hungry minnows.

"I won't," I said.

"I *am* like her. I can't stay here. I will outrun it, too." Her face was swollen on one side, darkening with bruises in the shape of an open hand. In my surprise, I released her and she dashed away, but I caught up to her again.

"Who did that?"

She knew what I meant, but she shook her head. She was beyond me.

My mind whirled, faster than the wind blew. I was sure that there were right words to say, if only I could find them.

"Eggshell," I yelled at her. "Will you leave her?"

Trouble stopped struggling. Her body trembled, suspended between choices.

"Running Woman abandoned Boulder," I went on. "Can you do the same to your sister?"

Trouble's eyes pleaded with me. She thought of a thousand answers that would permit her to go, but none of them were good enough. Her fury was a rock, thrown hard—then stopped against a wall.

"I can't be what they want." Her look was so powerful that it filled my eyes, and everything but her voice went very far away. For just that moment it was a house we lived in together in the most quiet clearing of the forest, or built on the top of a high hill. It was a look from which there was no joking escape, no turning away, no pretending not to understand.

"You are who you are, and no one but you can tell you the truth about that."

It was the porcupine's advice, but I was speaking it.

Trouble studied my face as if she were seeing it for the first time. "You listened," she said.

"I will never hit you," I told her.

CHAPTER EIGHT

 When Trouble and I entered my family's house, one of the guests, a very tall old man, was speaking, and he was doing it all wrong. For one thing, he was standing up while everyone else was seated. For another, he was talking too loud, as if noise alone would persuade people to understand.

For another, though he did not know any of us very well, still he stared directly into our eyes when he addressed us.

People were nervous and a bit impatient. They bowed their heads whenever his spiky words stopped. They frowned in concentration, as if they grasped whatever he was describing. They held back their laughter.

The man did not interrupt his speech when Trouble and I, wet from the sleet, moved to the fire to warm ourselves. We were invisible to him—but not to Mother. I knew her moods so well that I could follow the path of her thoughts: joy that I had come back, anger that I had gone at all, curiosity about Trouble's presence. Then, in the flickering light, my mother saw Trouble's cheek. She covered her mouth with the fingers of one hand and moved to sit beside us. Gently she lifted Trouble's tangled hair to better examine the bruise. She hummed softly, the way she comforted babies, and Trouble leaned against my mother's body, stiffly at first and then deeply, trying to fit herself into every curve.

Finally my mother glanced over at me. The scar

that divided her face was white as bone, white as lightning at night, as if her anger at what had happened to Trouble would crack her face. In answer, thunder boomed inside my head, and suddenly I was my mother's son in a more powerful way. Together we were the eyes and roar of a storm big enough to surround Trouble, to shelter her within our cool and windy circle. We looked at each other, Mother and I, and in that flash I was all the children she needed. I was enough.

The guest droned on and on. He unrolled a thin sheet of bark and waved it in front of his face. He patted his large stomach, full from eating too much food. He stretched one finger toward the ocean and then made rowing motions with his hands. "Ah," everyone responded, at last perceiving that this was a story about a boat!

Yes, yes, yes, the man nodded, happy that we appreciated him. He pointed to what remained of the feast, then to us, then to him.

"Ah," people said to each other. He was inviting us to come eat with them next time! But wait, there was more. "Ah!" His people *had* no food. We were

106

asked to come eat with them, but *we* were supposed to bring the meal. What an idea! I saw one uncle whisper a comment to another, and then they both hid their faces in their hands while their shoulders shook. Grandfather, however, seemed shocked. Clearly he had an opinion about this new custom that was not likely to be polite.

My father noticed his reaction also, and when the guest finally sat down, my father spoke before Grandfather had the opportunity.

"My son . . . ," he began, and looked at me in apology for what he was going to say next. "This morning, my son lost a story by accident. I wonder if he has found a new one to replace it? If he has, then this is the time to tell it to us."

***

Everyone turned toward me—even the guests, who watched what the rest of the people did and imitated them. I stared at my knees, my mind empty. What had my father done to me? Did he somehow know about the forest?

I listened for a story, shut my eyes and coaxed it like I sometimes tried to lure a suspicious but hungry mouse from its hole with an offering of corn set halfway between us.

"This old lady porcupine . . . ," I said, then stopped. The porcupine was my private story, and anyway, I hadn't made sense out of it yet. The mouse's shadow sank back into darkness.

I felt small within the bright light of many eyes and ears. Once started, a story couldn't be taken back, but I had nothing to say. The silence widened like a pool of spilled water.

"Excuse me," my mother said, amazing me with the sharpness of her tone. She was never comfortable talking in front of people outside her own clan, but . . . here she was, talking. "You've reminded me of a story I heard when I was a little girl. You must be tired, Moss, from gathering so much wood. You can tell us your new story at another time."

My mother was upset, but in such a covered-up way that only my father and I, who knew her voice best, could hear its shake. She coughed to clear her throat and, without waiting for me to answer, opened her hands on her knees, took a wide breath, and began.

***

THE BEAVER AND THE MUSKRAT WOMAN

There was a beaver who had a lodge on the shore of a swift river, and one day he was sunning himself on the bank when a muskrat woman came up to him.

"I need to go hunting on the other side," she said. "But I can't swim. Will you carry me across the water?"

"Of course," agreed the beaver, for he was hospitable and young, and happy to oblige.

So the muskrat woman climbed on his back and he set out. Though she was heavy, she was not too heavy, and soon the beaver had almost made it across.

"Wait," cried the muskrat woman. "I've forgotten my sack. We'll have to go back and get it at once."

The beaver sighed, took a wishful look at the dry land so close before him, then turned back. When he reached the place where they had begun, the muskrat woman hopped off, searched through a patch of reeds, found her sack, and hopped back on his back—forcing the air from his lungs in a loud blast.

"I'm ready," she announced, and once more the beaver set out, pushing against the water with his broad black

feet and arching his neck to keep his head above the surface. Now that the muskrat woman was a little wet, her weight seemed to have doubled.

The beaver struggled, for the current was swift, but shortly he was almost to a place where his webbed paws could touch the pebbly bottom.

"Oh dear," complained the muskrat woman. "I have left behind my needle and thread. I might need them. We'd better go back."

The beaver swiveled his head to look at her in hopes that she was making a joke, but she was already squinting her eyes toward the starting point.

"Hurry up. The good light will soon be gone." She tapped her sharp claws against the beaver's back to urge him to swim faster.

How easy it is to swim when I carry only myself, the beaver thought. It was an idea he had never had before.

When they reached the shore the beaver rolled onto his back and drew in great gulps of air while the muskrat woman rummaged again among the reeds.

"Right before my eyes!" she crowed, and held up a bone needle and a length of sinew thread before stowing them in her sack. "Your nap time is over. Let's go!"

The beaver, who normally slid into the waves so

smoothly that the only ripples came from the trail in the water left by his tail, flopped into the river with a huge splash. The muskrat woman was soaked, her fur had doubled its weight, but by closing his mind to every thought except how good it would feel to at last reach the far bank, the beaver managed to inch his way forward. Just when he was almost there, however, the muskrat woman spoke again.

"Silly me," she said. "I've brought everything with me that I need except what I need the most: my staff. How can I go hunting without that?" She pinched the beaver's ear and tugged it toward her. "Hurry up."

The beaver could endure no more and dived underwater. The muskrat woman gasped, then floundered and thrashed in the shallows, creating a great commotion. Somehow she managed to struggle herself onto the mud beach and dragged herself onto the clear spot of a bear path, where she sneezed and sputtered in anger.

"You said you'd help me!" she accused the beaver when he finally emerged, and angrily sank her teeth into his sensitive black nose. He was too exhausted by that time to fight back, so instead he just slipped back into the river and, weeping in pain, fought his way toward the other side.

***

Always before when I had heard this story it had been funny, causing people to laugh and smile. Today, for some reason, it was more serious. Perhaps it was the way Mother had told it. Perhaps it was the presence of the guests, who expected us to do everything for them and gave back little in return. They made us see ourselves as more like the too-helpful beaver than we would have liked.

It was by now very late at night. The fire had burned down into a circle of glowing red eyes that blinked and dimmed, ready, like us, for sleep. Father tapped two of the guests, gestured to the warmest mat in the house, then made a pillow of his hands and closed his eyes. Even they understood that idea and moved over to stretch out on the soft furs that had been spread for them. The rest of us took the far end of the room nearest the doorway.

But first my mother sent me to Trouble's house to let her family know she was safe with us. I walked across the dark clearing, listening to the music of the peepers calling out to each other. There was a half-moon, and in its silver light the forest rose all around the village like the dark, high sides of a bowl. Somewhere out there my porcupine was going about her business. Probably she had forgotten me—but I had not forgotten her. Her questions had been the beginning of the answers I needed to find about myself. I didn't know if today was enough of an away time for me. Perhaps I'd have to try again, be gone longer, and perhaps then I would meet a lynx or a bear. But they would not have more to teach me than the porcupine.

"You are who you are," she had said. To discover who I was, I didn't need to go away. I had to go *in*, and I had a feeling that was much more difficult. Maybe that was what Cloud had not been able to explain.

As I approached Trouble's house I heard the sound of angry voices, accusing each other.

"You drove her away," a woman said.

"You allow her to do anything," a man sneered back. "She must learn her place."

An older woman's voice interrupted. "Her place is here."

After a moment a small person came out of the

house and stopped when I whistled.

"Eggshell?"

"Moss?"

"Trouble is at our house. With my mother."

"I thought so. It's better, for now."

"Will you tell them?" It was strange to have a conversation outdoors at night. I couldn't see Eggshell's face, and so it was as if I were talking to everyone, to anyone.

"I don't think so. They'd just come get her. If they worry for a while . . . tomorrow will be calmer."

What must it be like to live in such a house? I thought of my father and mother, and their arguments seemed very small, very safe.

"Will they ask you?" I wondered if Eggshell would actually lie for her sister.

"I'm invisible," she said. "I'm the one like Boulder."

✳✳✳

All that night, my mother kept Trouble close by her side. She oiled and rebraided the part of Trouble's hair that had come undone, then she and Trouble spoke softly together long after the embers cooled down. I couldn't hear what they said, but I watched the silhouettes of their hands, their faces, for some clue. I could tell it was not the only time they had talked, and recalled that Trouble's family was related in some distant way to my mother's father.

Once, very late, Trouble pointed her hand to the place where I lay—they thought I was sleeping. She whispered into Mother's ear and immediately they both covered their mouths and bent low to the ground. They shushed each other, patted each other's backs. Their laughter was not unkind. I didn't mind it.

Father had stayed a long time outside, talking with his brothers and some of the other men. Before I had gone inside, I asked him a question that kept coming back to me.

"If the guests don't want to be guests and we don't want to be hosts, why did they come? Why did we ask them?"

"If only we could do just the things we wanted," my father said.

"Why can't we?"

"Because we're not alone in the world, Moss. This year, they needed us. They didn't want to need us, but they did. And next year . . . who knows? And so, we listen to need. We do what we are required. And sometimes it's not so bad."

I thought of the tall guest's proposal. "Do you think that next year we'll bring food to them?"

My father crooked his warm arm around my neck, hugged me to his chest. "Let the children of Never Enough dream," he said.

***

As dawn approached, Grandfather came quietly and lay beside me, his eyes open, the white parts bright as he gazed toward the smoke hole in the roof where now and then the flicker of northern lights splashed through.

"Where were you today, Moss?" he asked me.

I waited before I answered. He knew I had not been gathering wood—everyone realized that, of course—and I wanted to tell him the truth.

"I was in the forest," I said.

"What were you doing there?"

"I had an away time," I answered. "I think."

"You think?"

"Well, it seemed like that in some ways but not in others."

"How not?"

116

"It wasn't what I expected. It didn't last long. I didn't have a brave dream or meet a dangerous animal. There was a porcupine. . . ." I didn't know how to explain her. I thought of her quill, still in my pouch. "But Trouble showed up and we talked and came back home. I didn't change."

"You changed."

His words hung in the charcoal air. They hovered above me like a bird who has no fear. They were within my reach, but I was tired and I let them alone. Tomorrow he would explain to me what he meant.

"This porcupine . . . ?" he prompted.

"She was just an ordinary porcupine," I said. "Except . . . except she had no patience with my problems."

"Ah." I could almost feel Grandfather smile. "That one. What did she say?"

How did he know she talked to me?

"She made me tell me about myself."

"And . . . ?"

"I had to admit things I wasn't proud of: that I didn't want to be hospitable to the guests, that I wouldn't help get ready for them. That I was stubborn."

117

Grandfather suddenly became very busy with the bunched-up cloak he used as a pillow. He shifted his body, coughed, rubbed his teeth with a finger. Finally he spoke again.

"Surely there was more than that."

I remembered how the porcupine's words had echoed when I used them for Trouble. "She said I am who I am."

"Ah. And so you are. So are we all."

"But what does that mean?"

Grandfather reached across the darkness and touched my head. His hand was rough and soft at the same time. It was dry, large enough to cover my face in its protection. It smelled of smoke, of age, of Mother's soup, and when I breathed into it, the heat blew back and bathed me like a springtime breeze.

"You are your mother," Grandfather said. "You are your father. You are your brother and sisters who are gone before us. You are your grandmother who is annoyed with me but will forgive me." His voice caught and held.

"What about you?" I asked him. "Aren't I you, too?"

"Oh yes, Grandson. You are very much me." He

took back his hand, reached it high toward the sky as if to release my breath. "But most of all, you are you."

His words were like a gift hidden behind a tree, something that awaited me when I was ready to find it. I didn't want to ask too much, didn't want to show how little I understood, but there was one question I couldn't put off.

"What should I be as a man?" I asked him, and yawned as sleep called every part of me. I watched the last bits of shell white smoke rise toward the sky, joining together like a string of beads as they squeezed through the roof. Their patterns of light and dark were as difficult to decipher as the pictures that swim between stars.

"Ah," Grandfather sighed, getting comfortable as he thought about my last question. "Won't that be an interesting thing for us all to discover?"

My mind followed the smoke as it traveled high above the village. I dreamed the day, the swirls of faces, the high crest of trees. The porcupine's words, the guests arriving hungry, without their bowls. My father's arms. My mother's face. And Trouble, Trouble was a hunter and helped me find the story.